Planets, Plagues and Pandemics

Ray Filby

===

Planets, Plagues and Pandemics

Publisher : Midhurst

Published by Midhurst

Copyright © Ray Filby 2020

This is a work of fiction.
Any resemblance to actual persons,
living or dead, is purely coincidental.

Midhurst.
2, Freers Mews,
Warwick,
Warwickshire,
CV34 6DP

ISBN 978-1-9160485-8-4

http://midhurstpublishing.uk

<u>Acknowledgements</u>

The author would like to thank his wife, Sue, both for proof reading and for her patience and encouragement during the writing of these stories.

Contents

Introduction 9

Chapter 1 An Introduction to Klandacia 11

Chapter 2 The Culture and Politics of Klandacia 29

Chapter 3 The Mission Defined 39

Chapter 4 Preparation for the Mission 47

Chapter 5 The Voyage to Earth (Tromhem 5,3) 55

Chapter 6 The Moravian Church 60

Chapter 7 The Klandacians learn about the World's Problems 65

Chapter 8 The Klandacians are introduced to the World 79

Chapter 9 The World Tour 87

Chapter 10 An Encounter with Islamic Extremists 97

Chapter 11 Plans to effect a Rescue 113

Chapter 12 A Story with Two Endings 122

<u>Introduction</u>

Klandacia, a planet orbiting a nearby star, has a technology well in advance of that on earth. A pandemic, similar to the coronavirus outbreak experienced on earth, has caused the death of many Klandacians and is a recent memory to the humanoid population of this planet. As the Klandacians have developed an economy which is cashless, it came out of the pandemic without the economic turmoil experienced on earth as it emerges from the coronavirus pandemic.

The Klandacian Supreme High Priest receives a message from God requesting that help should be sent to earth. Although the journey to earth will take many years, four Klandacian astronauts volunteer for the mission, two men and two women. On reaching earth, the astronauts are able to acclimatise to earth's culture during a short time spent with a Moravian community, learning key languages they will need to communicate with the people on earth as they emerge from the pandemic. The Klandacians tour the world, providing useful advice and technology but experience one serious mishap before they are able to successfully complete their mission and return to their home planet.

Chapter 1

An Introduction to Klandacia

"We've been warned, our mission will be dangerous. Does this worry you? Does anyone want to pull out?"

Four young people were sitting in a park, thoughtfully contemplating what their future might hold as the evening gathered and the gloaming gave place to night. The night wasn't particularly dark however as illumination was provided by the three moons which orbited the planet. It was unusual for all three moons to be visible simultaneously but tonight, the two larger moons were almost in coincidence and the smallest moon would set beyond the western horizon in about an hour.

The person who had spoken was Stanilhem, a tall, thoughtful-looking, fair-haired young man.

"Naturally I'm apprehensive," answered Bramensel, a slim dark-haired young woman, "but I certainly wouldn't dream of pulling out of what promises to be an absolutely marvellous adventure and experience."

"Me neither," rejoined Karvilsel, the other young woman in the group. "I'm really looking forward to the mission and can hardly wait until we get clearance next week."

Karvilsel had shoulder length brown hair. She had an athletic figure and had the air of being a woman who liked to be in the thick of the action.

"I know how you like to be on the go most of the time. Will you be able to cope with being asleep ninety per cent of the time while we make this long journey?"

This question was posed by Gavilhem, the young man who was the fourth member of this quartet. Gavilhem had a sturdy build and the appearance of being a studious person. He considered the implications of what might happen before committing himself to rash action.

Our young people lived on a planet called Klandacia. The suffixes, 'hem' and 'sel' to their names distinguished male from female.

"Which star are we going to be headed to?" asked Karvilsel as the sky darkened and the stars became increasingly visible.

Gavilhem pointed to a constellation between the two larger moons and the small moon setting in the west.

"The star, Heston, is the one on the extreme right of Tromhem," said Gavilhem, using the name of the constellation which Karvilsel would recognise. Constellations visible from Klandacia had been given names of Klandacian men and women who were deemed to have given great service to the planet.

What was this inter-stellar mission which our young people were eagerly anticipating? Before explaining this, it is necessary to provide some key information about the planet Klandacia itself.

Klandacia had many similarities to our planet, earth. It was one of four planets which orbited a star somewhat larger than our sun. It was further from the star than earth is from the sun and thus, its year was just over six months longer than an earth year. It spun on its axis rather more slowly than the earth so that a Klandacian day lasted about twenty-seven hours. A Klandacian day, that is from midnight to the following midnight, or the period of rotation of the planet on its axis, was subdivided into twelve major time units (not 24 as on earth). A major time unit was further subdivided into twelve intermediate time units which in turn were subdivided into twelve minor time units. Thus, a Klandacian minor time unit corresponded fairly closely to an earth minute. A Klandacian week was seven Klandacian days. The fact that seven days corresponds to an earth week was not entirely a coincidence.

Thus, the make-up of a Klandacian year was as follows.

1 year = 70 weeks = 490 days.
1 year = 4 x 120 day seasons with 10 extra days.
The 10 extra days were split 2,3,2,3 between each season and were observed as public holidays.
1 season = 4 x 30 day months.

Although significantly larger than earth, the gravitational pull experienced on its surface was very close to that of earth's gravity. This was probably due to the incandescent core of the planet being less dense than that of earth, perhaps a higher proportion of aluminium and less of iron. Klandacia was the second smallest planet which orbited its star. The smallest planet in this particular solar system was very much closer to its parent star while the two larger planets orbited the star at the sort of distances that the planets Saturn and Jupiter are from the sun. The atmosphere of Klandacia was twenty per cent oxygen, seventy-four per cent nitrogen, five per cent argon and one per cent other gases like carbon di-oxide and water vapour. Thus, a human could survive very comfortably on Klandacia as could a Klandacian on the earth.

Plants and animals had evolved on Klandacia which had strong similarities to plants and animals on earth. The animal species could be subdivided into mammals, birds, reptiles and fish with just a small set of species whose life cycle was not totally different from the creatures we call amphibians. Countless species of invertebrate existed of which insect-like creatures were the most numerous. Almost all the insect-like creatures had brightly coloured wings but only a few had wings as large as butterflies or moths.

The four young people who will be the main subjects of this story were humanoid. Although their biochemistry was somewhat different from humans, there were only two markedly different external features. They had six toes on each foot and five fingers as well as the thumb on each hand. Hence, their system of counting and numerals was duodecimal, that is, there were twelve symbols to represent numbers including zero, and twelve would be written in a way which corresponds to our ten (10) and a gross as 100. *(If numbers occur in this narrative which are expressed in the Klandacian duodecimal system rather than the earth's decimal system, they will be written thus - 10 Kl, 60 Kl, 100 Kl)* Their century equivalent would be a gross of years. The life expectancy of a Klandacian was a Klandacian century (gross), most reaching this age but few living far beyond this. The other very unusual feature of Klandacians was their skin colour. This could be white or black or any colour between but unlike humans, their skin colour could change. The Klandacians would not know themselves what would be the colour of their skin when they woke in the mornings. Advanced as Klandacian science was, their scientists had no explanation for this phenomenon. When two Klandacians met for conversation, their empathy affected their hormones in such a way that their skin colours changed to be the same as each other. Thus, if a temporarily black Klandacian met a temporarily white Klandacian, the skins of both would change as they conversed until they were both the same colour brown!

The nature of Klandacian society was very special. Everyone had an overwhelming desire to do what was best for their neighbours. Thus, the society had no need of money! The role of some individuals in that society was to investigate everyone's needs and arrange for it to be supplied. This would include essentials like food, housing, furniture, entertainment, television, and utilities like electricity and water. Because of the generosity of members of that society, no-one went without for long. All their needs were supplied through the society around them and in this cashless society, no-one was greedy enough to make exorbitant demands on that society. On the contrary, the main desire of everyone was to be able to do things and follow careers which served and met the needs of others, whether this was in the nature of material things or providing services like teaching and health care or being entertainers. The Klandacians very much lived up to the ideal of everyone contributing to society according to their ability and only taking according to their need. People of academic prowess or professional seniority were not specially admired. The thing Klandacians most respected was the ability of an individual to provide special service to others.

As with our earth, geographically, the surface of Klandacia consisted of continents, islands and sea. There were nine continents and three-quarters of the planet's surface was covered by sea. The planet rotated about an axis which was sixty-five degrees to the plane defined by the planet's orbit about its star. Thus, the planet had the same sort of seasons as we experience on earth with ice-bound polar caps and a warm to hot tropical region. The land masses were covered by grassy plains, forests and jungles, mountains and deserts. A project which the Klandacians had been working on for over a couple of Klandacian centuries was the conversion of a huge desert, about the size of our Sahara, to arable land. They were well on with this project which included plans to leave a significant area as primeval desert which they recognised as having its own special majesty of space and silence.

The Klandacian roads in the countryside were beautifully landscaped dual carriageways. You would be driven rather than drive down these roads as the electric cars were programmed to self-drive their passengers to their selected destinations. On your journey, you would see very few buildings. These would mainly be hamlets of a dozen or so pretty cottages around a central farmhouse and a building for religious worship. The fields were abundant with crops or occupied by peacefully grazing animals which could be recognised as closely similar to the cows and sheep which are farmed on earth. Sometimes, you would encounter a few groups of very large and really majestic buildings set in parkland on the tops of gently rising hills. They appeared to be isolated but in fact, they were built above subterranean towns and cities and had very special functions, being worship centres, hospitals, sports stadiums and universities. There were always lots of people in the parkland around these buildings and these numbers could swell to crowds if special sporting or religious events were taking place in one of the buildings.

The sports stadiums hosted events which were much like those we enjoy on earth. Intercity and international events took place in these. An athletics event was very similar to the equivalent on earth with races over various distances, high and long jumping and throwing. Three different throwing events involved the use of balls of three different weights. There was nothing like putting the shot or throwing javelins and discus. These were lethal weapons reminiscent of what were used by the ancient Greeks and the civilizations with whom they competed as they fought wars over two thousand years ago on planet earth.

The Klandacians played a game called passball which was their equivalent of our football. It was played between two sides of twelve (10 Kl) on a hexagonal pitch. An inflated ball, very similar to a football, could be played by any part of the body including the hand, but only by a hand closed as a fist. The object of the game was to pass the ball to members of one's own side, attempting to string as many consecutive passes together as possible without the ball being kicked by a member of the opposing team. A point was scored by a side putting together as many as thirty-six (30 Kl) consecutive passes. Three points would be scored if the succession of passes could be increased to seventy-two (60 Kl). At each corner of the hexagon, coloured posts were placed, and two points could be scored each time a side managed to kick the ball to hit its own coloured post. The tactics of the game made it inadvisable to attempt to hit the post by kicking from too great a distance as if the ball missed and went out of play, the sequence of passes would be broken and the game restarted. This was done by the referee bouncing the ball in the centre spot and withdrawing a distance as the players, ranged round the edge of the centre circle, raced to get control of the ball. Electronic devices in the players boots and in the ball enabled the sequence of kicks to be automatically counted and displayed to the spectators on an electronic score board. The teams were enthusiastically cheered on by their supporters and a groan would go up from the supporters of a side where a pass had been intercepted by the opposition when the number of consecutive passes was getting near the point of achieving a score. The electronic scoring represented a great improvement in the game from the time when counting consecutive passes had been carried out by umpires on the touchline. Minor but good-natured disputes then arose if the opposition umpires believed that the passes had been miscounted. Variations of the game could be played between three teams of eight or four teams of six players when smaller numbers of consecutive passes were required to score points. However, the games between two teams were always the most popular and the better players were popularised, if not idolised, with pictures and posters on the walls of their supporters' bedrooms.

The Klandacian roads would not pass by the buildings located on the hilltops but were built so that as one approached the hills on which they had been constructed, the road would enter a tunnel which issued into an absolutely huge cavern. These caverns contained shopping areas, offices, factories, schools and dwelling accommodation for between sixty and a hundred and fifty thousand inhabitants. More than adequate car parking space was available. The roofs of these caverns were supported at intervals by large pillars within which fast moving lifts would convey people from the conurbation to the surface. The interior of these caverns was not at all gloomy. Illumination was provided by millions of light emitting diodes which had been selected so that in combination, they gave almost perfect white light, not the illusion of white light projected from some of the fluorescent lamps with which we are familiar on earth. The lights were located in the roofs of these caverns which were painted pale blue, and a gentle breeze was circulated through the caverns, giving a realistic illusion of being in the open air. As night approached on the planet surface, the light emitting diodes were programmed to gradually be turned off, leaving just sufficient lamps shining to enable safe navigation through the caverns. The simulated daylight enabled plant life to flourish and most of the houses had small gardens while the shops were arranged around elegant squares. As there was no rainfall within these caverns, artificial means of irrigating plant life had been set up. At the centre of many of the squares were beautifully carved statues celebrating Klandacians who had made a special contribution to the life of the planet. For example, in the main square at the centre of one of these conurbations were a pair of statues celebrating the husband and wife who had developed electro-magnetic induction nearly two thousand years earlier and were very much the parents of electricity as we know it. This couple were the equivalent of our Michael Faraday. Many statues celebrated great state presidents but there were none celebrating successful warlords. How could there be? War was unknown in Klandacia.

Near the larger towns were Klandacian airports. Conventional passenger terminals and radar towers for the air traffic controllers were evident but there were no runways. All Klandacian planes had been developed to take off vertically. Thus, airports were relatively compact.

Crime was unknown in Klandacian society but the streets were patrolled by uniformed individuals called wardens who were not there to prevent crime but to deal with the occasional traffic problem or contact the fire and ambulance services should an accident or event occur, requiring the intervention of the emergency services.

Klandacians were very environmentally conscious. Many more of the items, like the packaging which we just throw away on earth, were designed to be easily reused. Sophisticated recycling arrangements were available for most items that couldn't be reused. Almost everything was driven by electricity which was generated by a number of environmentally friendly means. Fossil fuels hadn't been used for several centuries. Nuclear power stations were driven by fusion rather than fission reactors. Klandacian scientists had abandoned research into nuclear fission when it was realised that a very destructive bomb was likely to be developed before the means of controlled fission could be established. It was realised that even when harnessed to generate electricity in a constructive way, nuclear fission would leave radioactive waste which would be difficult to dispose of.

Hydroelectric, wind and photoelectric power was generated in much the same way as it is on earth. Wind turbines had been built on remote islands out at sea and large areas of desert were covered with arrays of photocells. Hydroelectric power was generated, both from waterfalls and tides. The fact that Klandacia had three moons meant that tides were not the regular event they were on earth but ingenious methods of using irregular tides to generate electricity had been devised. As a material had been developed which was superconducting at ambient temperatures, there was no difficulty in transmitting low voltage electricity over vast distances from the location of generation to the point of use.

Geothermal energy was tapped by boring into the planets incandescent core from the mouths of extinct volcanoes and feeding pipes made of tungsten, and hence able to tolerate high temperatures, into the molten material beneath Klandacia's surface. The pipes were made in the form of u-tubes into which cold water was fed at one end and pumped through the tube to emerge as hot water or even as steam from the other end of the tube.

The most ingenious means of obtaining natural energy while at the same time, removing a planetary hazard, was a device which was able to harness the energy of tornadoes. On planet earth, tornadoes arise from the instability arising when the air near the earth's surface rapidly becomes hotter than the air in the layers above creating what may be referred to as a temperature inversion. Instead of the warm air rising by a gentle convection current, it suddenly convects, concentrating into the area of low pressure where the air initially started to rise, forming a vast, destructive, spiralling cone of fast-moving air. These tornadoes, often referred to as twisters, regularly devastate the southern states of America. This phenomenon may be thought of as the reverse of water spiralling down the plug hole as a bath is emptied. The Klandacians had developed a power generator which would move into the vast plains where tornadoes were likely to occur and precipitate the tornado by sucking up warm air from ground level into a column which accommodated large turbines. These would suck out the energy of the upward rushing warm air as it rushed to fill the vacuum created under the turbine column and thence up through the turbines. These generators were mobile and were moved across the plane to vacuum up as it were, the vast amount of energy stored in the temperature inverted air before it spontaneously and destructively erupted into a tornado at the impulse of nature.

Clearly, the Klandacians were well ahead of us earth in their technology and care of their environment but their culture and political systems brought further benefits to those living on the planet which we on earth can but envy.

Chapter 2

The Culture and Politics of Klandacia

In order to explain the mission for which our young people had volunteered, it is necessary to describe the religious and political organisation of Klandacia and its recent history.

Klandacia was divided into what might be seen to correspond to earthly nation states, each covering an area of about the same size as a major European state, France or Germany for example, and having a population between forty and a hundred million. Each state had its own government whose members were elected from the populations of the conurbations, the leaders of Klandacian religion and the managers of major Klandacian businesses. The conurbations had their own elected councils and, on occasions, some smaller units of local government were created in areas where special local needs had arisen.

Small religious buildings accommodating fifty or up to two hundred people existed within these caverns while the large cathedral-like buildings called temples which were built on the mounds above the inhabited caverns could accommodate between one and three thousand people, depending on the size of the particular conurbation being served. The smaller religious buildings, which were known in Klandacia by a name which means sub-temple, were overseen by one or sometimes two priests. The priests serving a conurbation would frequently meet as a chapter and elect between five and a dozen of their number to officiate at the main temple located above the ground. The officiants of groups of about forty sub-temples would elect members to represent them in the state government. Each nation state had its designated high priest.

Leaders of business units with over 144 (100 Kl) workers would also elect representatives to serve in the state government. The members of the state government elected a cabinet of ministers and the one who officiated as President of the state. The High Priest was an ex-officio member of the cabinet and was occasionally elected to occupy the dual role of High Priest and President.

Each nation state was represented on an organisation equivalent to our United Nations.

This body elected its own General Secretary with a five Klandacian year term of office. The High Priests of the nation states elected a Supreme Priest who was ex-officio on this body and had a similar five-year term of office. Supreme Priests were invariably very wise devout men or women who received clear messages from God during their times of prayer and they had considerable sway over decisions reached by this super-national council.

Klandacia was monotheistic and had only one religion but there were different traditions and forms of worship within that religion. Religious meetings included songs of praise, prayers, reading from scripture and comment. All were encouraged to contribute to these but it was customary for any who wished to speak to signify the fact to the officiating priest at the beginning of the service and the priest would control the order of events within the service. Funerals and weddings were conducted by priests at the sub-temples. Funerals were solemn and sad occasions as the mourners knew that they were saying farewell to a relation, friend or colleague who they would not see for some time, but they were no sadder than bidding farewell for someone who was moving to serve for some years in a distant country. The Klandacians had good reason through the revelations received by their priests to know that in time, they would join their departed loved ones in an even better world than Klandacia, Here they would directly experience the glorious presence of their God.

Many fewer Klandacians chose to get married than on earth but, as on earth, weddings were joyful celebrations. Divorce was very rare in Klandacia and could only take place during the first year of marriage if no children had been born or were expected. We would find the sole ground for divorce very strange. A person could divorce their spouse, with their agreement, if they sincerely felt they themselves had not come up to the standards they felt their husband or wife deserved and had a right to expect. The divorced spouse was then left free to marry someone to whom they might be better suited.

Klandacian scripture was a book of significant size but very much smaller than our Bible. It included an account of creation which was remarkably similar to our Genesis account with seven epochs being defined, the seventh one being the epoch during which God rested. Hence the Klandacians celebrated the seventh day of their week as a sabbath rest day. The scripture also included an account of the establishment of organised Klandacian religion and guidance on performing acts of worship, a large set of worship songs, and books giving guidance on the getting the best out of life. Sin as we know it on earth didn't exist in Klandacia but misadventures did occur. These were not the result of malicious action but due to carelessness or lack of sound judgement. Some Klandacians were particularly accident prone. Although a cashless society, Klandacians understood the concept of property and although robbery was unknown, disputes sometimes arose which, in the end, usually turned out to be the result of someone forgetting to return a borrowed item. Similarly, murder was unknown but careless acts sometimes led to what on earth would be called manslaughter. The Klandacians were aware that there was a force for evil and this had been at work during creation interfering with God's intentions. This force was responsible for the creation of harmful bacteria and viruses and also for the evolution of vile creatures like venomous snakes. Some Klandacian philosophers argued that, had there been no force of evil interfering in the process of creation, carnivorous animals would never have come into existence. This force for evil was behind natural disasters like earthquakes, volcanoes, tsunami and hurricanes which were timed to create maximum death and devastation to disrupt Klandacian life.

The Klandacians were warned that the force for evil was out there, just looking for an opportunity to take over a Klandacian life. One book in Klandacian scripture was a parable of a Klandacian whose life had been taken over by this force for evil. He committed robbery and murder to amass personal possessions, but these ultimately resulted in his self-destruction. Fortunately, this occurred before he could procreate. This parable was the only example of real sin of which the Klandacians would become aware and they were warned by their priests that any descendants of a person who had committed such sin would themselves have been tainted with sin with disastrous consequences for the whole of the Klandacian race! The Klandacians were a contented people and none had the slightest urge to commit real sin by thought, word or deed.

A disaster of recent memory which had devastated Klandacia was a pandemic which had severely reduced the planet's population. This had occurred ten years earlier and took the form of narcolepsy, a sleeping sickness. An individual would be overcome with extreme drowsiness. They couldn't be kept awake and would have to sit down wherever they were and they would then fall into deep slumber. There was no means by which the sleeping individual could be awakened and after about eighteen Klandacian hours, they would either peacefully pass into death or awake, feeling comfortably rested. Fortunately, by far the most individuals afflicted with this sleeping sickness would awake and, by and large, it was only the elderly who would pass into death, but the disease was no respecter of age or gender. Equal numbers of men and women died and individuals as young as twenty had died. The disease was extremely infectious and only a rigorous policy of self-isolation could slow its progress. In this way it was very similar to the coronavirus pandemic which we have experienced on earth. Klandacian technology was well advanced and many could work from home. Manufacturing was largely carried out by robots which could be programmed and controlled from home with only a few operatives needed on the factory floors. Essential workers, including medical staff, continued to work. Food production continued in the countryside where the risk of encountering an infected person was very much less and the Klandacian equivalents of supermarkets remained open. However, most people received their food by pre-ordered delivery. It took six months for the Klandacian scientists to develop a vaccine against this disease and from then onwards, things quickly returned to normal.

What was the economic impact of this disaster? In a cashless society, economics doesn't have the same significance as in our highly commercial world and there was hardly any short or long term impact on Klandacian society. Businesses had not become bankrupt. No-one had lost money. No-one had money to lose! During the outbreak, entertainment in the form of theatres and sporting events had not taken place and most shops were closed. However, people were adequately fed, the many television channels provided entertainment and people could catch up on their reading. Directions were given to parents on how to continue to educate their children. The provision for face to face contact and conference call by computer was rather better than we have now on earth through packages like Skype and Zoom. Thus, at the end of the Klandacian pandemic, things quickly returned to normal without the economic consequences experienced in a commercially orientated society.

While mobile phones are ubiquitous on earth, Klandacians had something better. They all carried a pocket computer which could be folded or even screwed up like a handkerchief and stored in one's pocket. Should one wish to use this computer, one would take it from ones pocket and magnetically attach a small box which was about two inches square and one inch thick, This box contained the computer's solar charged battery, its operating system and memory. Within seconds of attaching the power supply, the previously floppy sheet would become a rigid sheet just over the size of what we know as an A4 sheet of paper. A touch sensitive keypad and menu would be on display and it was thus ready to be used as computer much as we might operate a lap-top computer. It included functions which enabled it to be used as a camera or a phone.

Klandacian technology was obviously well ahead of earth technology. How long had it taken this technology to develop? If we measure the development time of civilization from the time that primitive writing and reading started to be used, it has taken about four thousand years for earth's technology to develop to its present state. It had taken the Klandacians nearer six thousand years to reach the current state of development on the planet, but after four thousand years, their technology hadn't developed much beyond that of mediaeval Europe. War and the acquisition of wealth were stimuluses which accelerated the development of earth's technology. In the absence of war and the insatiable desire for wealth and status, things had developed at a much more leisurely rate on Klandacia and without the collateral damage to the planet which would have come with war.

Chapter 3

The Mission Defined

The Council of Nations was in session. The Supreme Priest had an important matter to bring before the Council.

A hush fell over the assembly as Supreme Priest Lamethem rose to his feet at the bidding of the Council's General Secretary. Lamethem had a tall, austere figure, white, shoulder length hair and a short beard. He wore a plain, long yellow robe tied at the waist with a green sash. This was the garb worn by all Klandacian priests and carried no feature to indicate the status of the wearer. Klandacians were not a status conscious people.

"Last night, I dreamed that as I stood amongst you, the Klandacian Council of Nations, I saw a crowd of people who were calling to us,

"Come and help us!"

"Who are you and where are you from?"
I asked.

The people faded and a constellation which I recognised as Tromhem came into view and then this faded.

Later that night, I had exactly the same dream except that when I asked who they were and where they came from, a single star appeared with a family of planets. Later still that night, the dream was repeated but this time, when the star and planets appeared, the vision zoomed into the third planet out from the star. There was no further recurrence of the dream but the dream was so vivid and as it recurred three times, each time revealing more of the location of those who were calling, it cannot be dismissed as just a dream. I believe that God is revealing to you through myself, a planet which we are being called upon to help."

For a moment, there was silence among the councillors and then they began to talk excitedly among themselves. Lamethem sat down. The General Secretary raised his hand to hush the gathering and then spoke himself.

"It is quite clear to me that God has spoken to us through Supreme Priest Lamethem and we are now faced with a challenge to which we must respond. Can anyone give us more information about the planet which appeared in Lamethem's dream and make suggestions as to how we might respond to this challenge?"

One of the councillors rose to his feet.

"From Supreme Priest Lamethem's description, it is likely that the star in question is Heston, the fifth brightest star in the constellation Tromhem, for this is the only star in that constellation which we know has more than two orbiting planets. If the planet is the third one out from its star, it will be referenced in the scientific journals as Tromhem 5,3. As to deciding how we might respond to the challenge, I think we must first consult our scientists who can tell us more about that planet."

It was agreed that the Council should recess and meet again in three days when a prominent astronomer could be available to provide more information about this planet. It was also suggested that the presence of the International Director of Space Research should be requested to comment on the feasibility of carrying out a mission to Tromhem 5,3.

Three days later the Council reconvened with Professor Jonamsel, a prominent astronomer, and Director Vandahem, who was in charge of space research, present.

Professor Jonamsel was able to give the information requested about Tromhem 5,3. It had been the subject of observation from the huge telescope which orbited Klandacia well above the Klandacian atmosphere and could thus provide very clear and detailed pictures. She reported that it was a slightly smaller planet than Klandacia and had a similar atmosphere to Klandacia. The length of its day and year were shorter than that of Klandacia but its surface temperature was much the same and thus, it appeared to be an environment in which a Klandacian could safely exist.

Director Vandahem was not optimistic about the chance of launching a successful mission to Tromhem 5,3 but did not rule it out as impossible.

"Tromhem is eight lightyears away," he reported. "We have a large space station currently orbiting Klandacia which could be used for the mission, but it will only accommodate four people. The maximum speed to which we could accelerate such a station if taken out of orbit and directed towards another star would be about eighty percent of the speed of light. This means it could take up to twelve years to reach Tromhem. Do we have competent astronauts who would be prepared to spend twelve years there and another twelve years to get back, cooped up in a space station?"

Professor Jonamsel pointed out that drugs could be provided which would cause a drop in the astronauts' temperature and enable them to sleep for months at a time in a state of suspended animation. After three months, they would need to reawaken for a few hours to take nourishment and see to other bodily functions before returning to an extended pattern of sleep.

Director Vandahem provided further information.

"If any suitable astronauts volunteered for such a mission, they could be launched in a space capsule programmed to automatically dock on to the space station. This capsule could be used to land on Tromhem 5,3 as it was designed to enter a planet's atmosphere gently so that it wouldn't burn up and thence, it could be controlled like a plane to make a safe landing. However, apart from what Professor Jonamsel has told us about the planet, our telescopes are not yet powerful enough to give us much information about the planet's surface. We do know that regions on that planet glow during the planet's night, suggesting that whoever occupies the planet can create artificial light but that's about all. I feel we owe it to whoever is to undertake this mission to provide some guidance on where they might land safely."

Supreme Priest Lamethem then rose to his feet.

"This is a problem which has perplexed me. I agree that we must take a responsible attitude towards the safety of any who are brave enough to undertake this mission but there is another dimension for us to take into account. We are not considering embarking on this expedition simply as an enterprise in space exploration. My visions clearly came from God and He can be trusted to support any efforts we make ourselves to respond to His message. We must undertake this enterprise in partnership with Him and He will see to any details which are beyond our ability to discern, including arranging for the space capsule to find a safe and suitable landing site. This means that we should embark on this venture prayerfully for there is so much that could go wrong if we just rely on ourselves and the technology we have at our disposal. I suggest that we now spend some time in prayer and that as we return to our nation states to report on what is being considered, we urge our own people to enter into prayer partnership for the success of this mission."

A silence fell over the council and then various members spoke as they felt led. They prayed first that it should become abundantly clear to all Klandacians that this was a mission which God had laid on their hearts to undertake. Secondly, they prayed that the right astronauts should be selected to fulfil this mission and that they should be protected throughout by God. This included prayer that God should direct them to a safe landing place on Tromhem 5,3, and that they would return safely, able to report on a successful outcome of their mission.

After a while, there were no further contributions to the prayers being offered and Supreme Priest Lamethem closed the prayer session.

Director Vandahem then rose to make a final statement. As I am responsible for space research, it is incumbent on me to identify the most suitable astronauts to undertake this work. This selection is so important that it cannot be hurried but I hope to be able to find the right people within a fortnight.

The General Secretary of the Council of Nations closed the meeting. The delegates dispersed, excited by this challenge but apprehensive of how it might turn out for the astronauts who would actually undertake this mission.

Chapter 4

Preparation for the Mission

Immediately on returning to his office at the Klandacian Space Research Headquarters, Director Vandahem set about making preparations for this great mission. He first needed to identify the team of astronauts who would be prepared to undertake this hazardous enterprise. He had suitable individuals in mind but didn't want to impose this task on any but the most willing volunteers and he advertised around the various centres from which astronauts operated, explaining the importance of the mission, that it was being set up in response to a divinely promoted message received by Supreme Priest Lamethem and that it would mean spending at least twenty-four years away from Klandacia. He made sure that the applicants would be aware of the danger and discomfort associated with the mission. He also pointed out that due to a consequence of relativity known as time dilation, when they returned, their contemporaries on Klandacia would have aged considerably more than they had done because they would have spent years in a space station, travelling at great speed. Vandahem invited applicants to reply with a list of qualifications, an account of their experience and a letter explaining both why they wished to be involved in this mission and why they felt that they would be suitable for the job.

Many more applications were received than Vandahem had expected but as you know from the first chapter of this story, Stanilhem, Bramensel, Karvilsel and Gavilhem were the ones selected. Vandahem was particularly pleased that these were among the applicants so keen to go on this mission for a number of reasons. He was already familiar with them as individuals and knew that they had an excellent reputation for reliability, initiative and hard work. Most important of all, they related well to those around them and already knew each other as they were all based at the main space research station in Klandacia. Whatever their technical ability may been, it would have been a great mistake to recruit an individual who was unlikely to get on with his or her colleagues and be unable to cope with being in their limited company over an extended period of time. The four successful applicants were young enough so that, in Klandacian terms, they would not be particularly old when they returned and they had already experienced extensive journeys of exploration in space stations. Each one had been on voyages around the two large planets in Klandacia's particular solar system.

Naturally, this quartet were both excited and apprehensive as they attended briefing sessions with Vandahem and other senior members of the Space Research Station staff. They would be breathing, eating and drinking, air, food and water reconstituted from their own waste products. To most of us on earth, this sounds totally distasteful but our astronauts had already experienced this during their long journeys to the outer planets of their system and knew that it wasn't as bad as all that. The food and water were hygienically processed and had powders and tablets added to ensure that they were not only nutritious but tasted good and wholesome and contained the requisite vitamins. The atmosphere in the space station was circulated through an electro-chemical device which converted the carbon dioxide, generated as they breathed, back into oxygen and fed the carbon back into the food chain. Thus, the astronauts always had fresh air to breathe.

They would have to take tablets which would cause their temperature to drop and they would fall asleep for three months at a time. They were assured that unlike the sleeping sickness that had afflicted the planet some ten years earlier, there was no malignant virus or bacteria in these tablets. They would wake feeling relaxed and refreshed. It was important that they all took these tablets at the same time so that they would wake at about the same time and enjoy each other's company for a few hours when they would see to necessary housekeeping and personal hygiene. They were advised to load their handkerchief computers with books and films to provide entertainment on the journey and also to have films of Klandacia which would be useful to show to the inhabitants of Tromhem 5,3. They all had experience of docking on to the space station in their space capsule and also of entering the planet's atmosphere while travelling in the space capsule when their mission was over and they were returning home. However, what and where their landing site on Tromhem 5.3 might be were imponderables. All they could be told was that this was a divinely sponsored mission and God could be trusted to guide them to the right place.

As the space capsule operated as a vertical take-off and landing plane, they would have some control themselves in steering the capsule to a flat space to land.

As you can imagine, the quartet had many excited discussions about the mission and speculated what Tromhem 5,3 would be like and how they might relate to the inhabitants. Bramensel had giggled at the notion that on their return, her young brother would be physically older than herself. Their parents had mixed feelings about their offspring embarking on such a mission which would mean their spending many years away from their families as they journeyed to a destination about which they knew nothing. They were proud that these members of their families had been selected to represent the planet on this extraordinary mission but they felt overwhelming sadness that their loved ones would be away for so long to say nothing of the anxiety they experienced through fearing that they might not return. Because of the vast distances involved, even radio communication would not be possible.

It will be of interest to the reader to know something about the space station in which they would be travelling. This was currently in orbit around Klandacia but once it had left Klandacian space, computers on board would successfully steer it to a suitable orbit around Tromhem 5,3 at the end of their journey. It was powered by a nuclear fusion reactor and there was more than enough hydrogen on board to take them many times to the Heston solar system and back to Klandacia. Once the space station had been accelerated to the required speed, it would keep on going without needing any further input from the station's energy which would then be used just for lighting and other domestic purposes required by our astronauts in the space station.

The space station itself was a vast hollow toroid (doughnut shape) with hollow cylindrical passageways leading from one side of the toroid to the other and intersecting at the centre. The special point about the space station being constructed thus is that it could be kept spinning so that those within the toroid would experience simulated gravity. Our astronauts would walk around the outer perimeter of the toroid, their bodies orientated radially to the space station's geometry, that is, with their heads towards the centre of the space station. The cylinders which crossed the diameter of the space station had handles on the walls which would aid the astronauts as they climbed through these tunnels to traverse the space station. The outward pull of the centrifugal force generated by the spinning space station would get less as they reached the centre and then increase as they climbed down to the opposite wall the other side of the station.

After further training and simulation of some of the operations which they would have to carry out on the voyage, the day of the launch finally arrived. Huge crowds had gathered at the Klandacian Space Research Headquarters to wish our astronauts well and to witness the historic event which this launch represented. They were hugged by the International Council's General Secretary and Supreme Priest Lamethem. The General Secretary made a speech of encouragement and hope. Supreme Priest Lamethem prayed for their safety and for the success of the mission and added that they would have the peace of knowing that God, although unseen, was with them in a very real way as they sought to fulfil His mission. After this, our astronauts proudly walked across to the space capsule and settled into the seats inside. They were not wearing the sort of space suit that we are familiar with as the garb of astronauts leaving earth but smart specially designed suits which could be worn as normal apparel while on the surface of Klandacia, carrying out their usual duties. Special space suits were not required as throughout the flight, it was expected that both in the capsule and the space station, our astronauts would be breathing the air contained in those environments. Space suits were available within the space station in the event of there being a need to leave the station to effect an external repair. The astronauts had been trained in how this might be done in their course of being prepared for this mission.

The people waited in silence until the usual countdown was complete and erupted into a great cheer as the capsule was launched into space. Their parents watched in proud silence but the mothers could not resist shedding a tear as the capsule carrying their children disappeared into the sky, not knowing when or if they would ever see them again.

Chapter 5

The Voyage to Earth (Tromhem 5,3)

After the capsule's successful launch, it completed its journey to the orbiting space station and the robot system on board the capsule guided it to dock on to the space station. The four astronauts transferred to the mother ship and began to take stock of what would be their home for the next twelve years. Stanilhem, who was the designated pilot for the group, operated the control which launched them on their journey and the spacecraft accelerated out of its orbit round Klandacia. A trajectory had been chosen which passed the two large planets which were part of the star's solar system, using the pull of these planet's gravity to add to the space craft's acceleration. They watched with awe as Klandacia receded to be seen as just a small sphere. In due course, the larger planets would loom up in turn as huge spheres and then, these too would recede as the spaceship set off on its interstellar journey.

In their excitement, they had hardly eaten before leaving their friends and family to enter the capsule which had taken them to the space craft. The departure was not unexpectedly emotional. Their mothers had shed a few tears. Their fathers stoically expressed their pride that they had been chosen to be the pioneers who would undertake this ground-breaking mission. Their siblings looked on in awed silence. No-one expressed the fear or even believed they would not return safely. The astronauts now prepared a meal from the spacecraft's larder and reminisced on the past few weeks training.

They had been carried by their adrenalin to this point but now the reality of what they were undertaking came home to them. Bramensel and Karvilsel shed a few tears with the realisation that it would be twenty-four years before they saw their families and friends again. Stanilhem and Gavilhem did their best to comfort the young women but were not far from tears themselves.

After clearing the meal away, they spent a little time reading books they had loaded on to their handkerchief computers and then took the tablets which would lower their temperatures and enable them to sleep continuously for three months. They had complete confidence in the spacecraft's computerised navigation system to see them safely on their way.

After the three months had elapsed, Gavilhem was first to awake but within an hour, the others revived to share his company. They were hungry and shared a really good meal together. They spent the next few hours looking out at the stars, playing board and card games, watching a film and reading. As they surveyed the vast universe from their rotating spacecraft window, the stars looked very different from their appearance from the surface of Klandacia. They were sharp points of light set against a pitch-black sky. The stars in the Milky Way (yes, their home star was part of the same galaxy as our earth) could be seen as separate entities and not as part of a vast haze of light. The star they had left appeared itself as rather more than just a pinpoint of light but they knew this would soon recede to become indistinguishable from the other stars. Karvilsel prepared a warm drink and they took the pills which would enable them to hibernate for another three months.

The next twelve years were uneventful and followed much the same pattern. The foursome had been well chosen. They remained good company for one another right through the voyage. They were well educated beyond the scientific skills which particularly fitted them for this mission and entered into stimulating conversations with one another, covering topics which ranged from the fauna and flora of Klandacia to the history and geography of the planet. During their waking hours, they read passages together from their holy book and spent time in prayer, remembering those back home and petitioning God to help them fulfil the purpose for which He had sent them. They exercised by walking several times round the perimeter of the spaceship.

At last, as almost twelve years had elapsed, they realised that they were directly approaching a star which was enlarging on their field of vision. This was Heston (or Tromhem 5) which we would call our sun. They took in with awe the giant outer planets as they passed them by, showing particular interest in the rings around them and being specially impressed with the spectacular concentric system of rings circulating Saturn. The spacecraft's computerised guidance system took them into orbit around the third planet out and they excitedly prepared to enter the space capsule.

Once settled and strapped into their seats, Stanilhem separated the capsule from the mother ship. They took a deep breath and started their descent to the earth's surface. They safely entered the earth's atmosphere from which point the capsule could be operated like a plane. Some of the earth's military radar system picked up an unidentified aircraft which seemed to be heading for central Europe and jets were scrambled to intercept it but it had landed well before any aircraft had come near it and the jets returned to base when they were ordered to abort their mission.

No-one had any idea where the plane would land. The Klandacian Supreme Priest said that as they were on His mission, God would direct them to a suitable landing point. Stanilhem identified a green square surrounded by houses which he decided would be a good position to land. He switched the controls to vertical landing mode and they put down gently into the centre of this square.

Chapter 6

The Moravian Church

Pastor Bergenstadt was the minister of a flourishing church in the part of the Czech Republic known as Moravia. His community, like nearly every other community on earth, had suffered as a result of the Coronavirus pandemic. They were now emerging from this worldwide disaster. Strict social isolation was no longer being enforced. Vaccinations were now becoming available. Many of Pastor Bergenstadt's flock had contracted this disease. Several had died. Most had recovered. The whole community had not been tested to ascertain just how many people had been infected and how many had escaped. Thus, it is likely that some had contracted the disease without showing any symptoms.

The problem now being faced by post-coronavirus communities was an economic one. Many had become unemployed. Businesses had collapsed.

Pastor Bergenstadt arranged a meeting with his church elders. It was decided that they should determine as far as possible what had been the economic impact on members of their church during this period. Just how many thousands of pounds (or their Czech equivalent) would be needed to set the dispossessed back on their feet and to revive businesses. It was discovered that the losses incurred varied from five to thirty thousand pounds. Fortunately, most of the members of the church had not lost out financially as they were either able to remain in normal employment or work from home. Indeed, some had actually become better off as a result of this pandemic because they were in businesses which manufactured protective equipment for health workers. Others were a little more wealthy than before because they'd been unable to spend money over the period of social isolation. However, the distress experienced by many was dire.

Once the figures had been gathered in, they were analysed by the church treasurer who reported that allowing for the financial compensation available from the government, much of which was just available in the form of loans, about ninety-five thousand pounds would be needed meet the debts that had been incurred by the worse affected and get businesses up and running again. This figure was significantly less then Pastor Bergenstadt had feared.

Another meeting of the elders was convened at which it was decided to tell the church the sum of money that would be needed to support their members facing pecuniary difficulties as a result of the pandemic and that it was planned to hold a gift day when the money raised would be used to help its members facing financial problems. Pastor Bergenstadt reminded them that the early church in Jerusalem had done something very similar to ensure that its poorer members did not suffer undue hardship. A prayer meeting would be held before this gift day. Pastor Bergenstadt was optimistic. He had a truly spiritual congregation and many were not only wealthy but had not been adversely affected by the economic recession caused by the pandemic. Pastor Bergenstadt was not disappointed. A sum of money just short of one hundred thousand pounds was raised on the gift day. The extra money would be needed because no-one had overestimated their losses and it was feared that some had grossly underestimated what they might need to get back to normal.

A week after the gift day, Pastor Bergenstadt had a dream. In the dream, a voice had clearly told him that visitors from another planet would arrive at his church. They were not angels but real people, very similar to humans, and they would be in a position to help the world as it emerged from the effect of this pandemic. While members of the church would have to know about these extra-terrestrial visitors, their presence was not to be widely broadcast beyond church members until they had had time to acclimatise themselves to earth and learn about the earth's problems and culture. To enable these visitors to provide the help which they could give to the world's population, they would need to learn the languages they would require to effectively communicate their wisdom.

Pastor Bergenstadt communicated the details of what he realised had been a divine communication to his elders. They were allowed to share this information with other church members with the instruction that the arrival of these visitors was not to be publicised. Two days later, the space capsule landed on the green near the Moravian church. The houses around the green were largely occupied by Moravian church members who were not totally surprised at this arrival from outer space but were nonetheless very excited. They flocked out on to the square to meet the four Klandacians as they emerged from their capsule.

Chapter 7

The Klandacians learn about the World's Problems

The Klandacians emerged from their capsule, blinked in the sunlight and stood regarding the circle of people standing around them in awed silence. Pastor Bergenstadt and his wife, Margarite, stepped forward to meet them. How should they greet these strangers? It wasn't wise or appropriate to rush forward to hug them. Was handshaking a customary gesture for these people? In the end, they just made a small bow, gave them a warm smile, stood to one side and gestured to the fine manse by the church on one side of the square. They then led the way forward, followed by the Klandacians.

How does one start to communicate with people from a totally different culture while not knowing their language? The first thing to do was to make them feel comfortable and at home. Pastor Bergenstadt and Margarite conducted them into their spacious dining room and removed a couple of chairs from the round table leaving just six. They had been expecting the arrival of these guests but had no idea how many there would be. Pastor Bergenstadt gestured them to be seated and then went out to the kitchen with Margarite, returning with plates of ham salad, rolls and butter, together with glasses of water which they set before the Klandacians. They then returned with cutlery which they laid beside each plate and finally, brought in their own food and settled into the remaining chairs themselves. Pastor Bergenstadt put his hands together, looked up to heaven and said his customary short grace. He realised of course that this would mean nothing at first to the Klandacians but knew that thy would be closely observing everything they could to learn about the customs of this different race among whom they had come to live.

"I am <u>Bergenstadt</u>," he said, pointing to himself, "and this is <u>Margarite</u>," he continued, pointing to his wife.

This was a good start. Stanilhem introduced the members of the group.

"Bramensel, Karvilsel, Gavilhem," he said pointing to each of his companions in turn and finally to himself, "Stanilhem,"

Pastor Bergenstadt picked up his knife and fork as did Margarite and started to eat. The Klandacians observed closely, tentatively picked up their cutlery, looked up again to see just how they were being used, and then started to eat themselves. After they had taken just a few mouthfuls, Bergenstadt and Margarite were relieved to see they were eating with relish and enjoying their food. Although they would have preferred to provide their visitors with a hot meal, Bergenstadt and Margarite had decided that it was important to provide their visitors with good food as soon as they arrived and although their arrival was not unexpected, they had had no prior indication as to the actual day or hour of the Klandacians arrival.

After they had all finished the salad course, Bergenstadt and Margarite cleared the plates away and brought in bowls of steamed pudding which they had heated in the microwave. The Klandacians enthusiastically devoured these. Finally, they served mugs of hot coffee. The Klandacians could feel the mugs were warm and sipped their drinks very carefully. They were visibly becoming more relaxed as they began to become acclimatised to this new home.

After the meal, Bergenstadt conducted the Klandacians to the main living room of the house, gestured for them to sit in the armchairs and finally sat down himself. A short while later, Margarite joined them. Up until now, apart from the initial introduction when they shared their names, everything had been done in almost silence. Bergenstadt realised that he must now start to develop meaningful communication with his guests, and with gestures, sounds and drawing on paper, they started to make good headway. They discovered that the Klandacians had travelled over a long period of time from a planet which was one of a family of four, orbiting a distant star.

As the evening started to draw in, Bergenstadt and Margarite realised that the Klandacians would be getting tired. As they had no idea of how many guests would be arriving, they had prepared several guest rooms in their ample sized manse and conducted them upstairs to the bedrooms. They indicated which was their own room and gestured for the Klandacians to choose which rooms they would like for themselves. There were two rooms with twin beds and six single rooms. The Klandacians chose the two twin rooms for themselves. Unlike the single rooms, these each had a toilet and shower en suite. The two men chose one of these rooms and the girls the other.

Bergenstadt and Margarite suddenly became aware that their guests would have no night attire and quickly hustled up a selection of pyjamas and nightdresses, having no idea what Klandacians usually wore at night. The Klandacians realised what they were being shown and they all chose a pair of pyjamas each. Bergenstadt showed them how the lights and curtains worked and left their guests to settle in for the night and get some sleep. As soon as the Klandacians had realised they were approaching the bright star which must have been Heston (Tromhem 5), their destination star, they had ceased to take the tablets which had left them sleeping for three months at a time so that, although they were now enjoying a more natural sleeping pattern, it would be a welcome change to sleep in a comfortable bed. When alone in their separate rooms, the Klandacians expressed to each other their great delight that they had been divinely directed to this particular home. It exceeded their wildest expectations. Bergenstadt and Margarite similarly expressed to each other their pleasure that they had been selected to host these very special extra-terrestrials.

The next day, after they had all enjoyed a good cooked breakfast, Bergenstadt invited one of his church members, Merbrandt, to join them. Merbrandt had served as a pioneer missionary among primitive tribes living in the Amazon basin and had developed skills in communicating with people of totally unknown languages. He was adept at both learning these languages and teaching his own. Merbrandt, together with Bergenstadt and Margarite, spent the next few days in getting to know the Klandacians and teaching them to speak and write in the Czech (Bohemian) language. They were impressed by how rapidly they picked this up. This was remarkable in view of the fact that Klandacia was a monolingual planet, (there had been no Tower of Babel event on Klandacia) and the quartet had therefore no previous experience of different languages.

After about only two weeks, it was realised that the Klandacians could follow the language well enough to understand most of what was happening at a church service. Thus, that Sunday, the Klandacians attended the morning service at Pastor Bergenstadt's church next door. By that time, they had already been introduced to several senior members of that congregation. The main congregation had been told in advance that although naturally curious about these extra-terrestrial visitors, they should not throng round them but approach them with courteous dignity. The Klandacians obviously enjoyed the lively service and mentally compared it with the sabbath worship which took place on their own planet. There were many similarities.

During these early weeks, the Klandacians learnt much about life on earth and Bergenstadt and members of his church, who were invited to spend time with them, learned about Klandacia. As Klandacia and its customs were explained, Bergenstadt realized that this was not just a planet whose technology was advanced beyond that on earth but that it had not experienced the fall and its people were free from what we on earth recognize as sin. The parable from their Holy book about the man who had committed robbery and murder and had finally destroyed himself was the story of a person who, had he procreated, would have been a Klandacian Adam, infecting the whole planet with sin. Sin and the way it affected the world was quite difficult to explain to the Klandacians. Money was also a foreign concept to the Klandacians who lived in a cashless society.

Money was explained as something which was quite neutral in itself but depending on how it was used, it could lead to either good or bad outcomes. Money was greatly desired because it conferred power on the owner, power to purchase possessions and hire the services of other men and women. As a result of individuals having different abilities to acquire money, great disparities in society had arisen as a result of the different amounts of wealth that individuals had acquired. Society tended to look up to those who had most money and could display this wealth by the possessions they owned, their houses, their cars, their clothing and additional things like jewellery. This amazed the Klandacians as it was totally alien to the culture of their home planet.

"Yes," they were told, "money itself was neither good or bad but the Bible, which was described to the Klandacians as a gift from God to enable those on earth to know more about him, taught that the love of money was the root of all evil things."

It was explained with great care that everyone living on the planet they were visiting was infected to a greater or lesser degree by the sin they had inherited from their forefather, Adam. There was nothing they could do in their own strength to overcome this sin and as a result, there was a gulf between themselves and God which did not exist for the Klandacians. God was aware of this and had come to earth in human form to remove this gulf. The appointed way to atone for sin had been to offer sacrifice to God but the animal sacrifices were imperfect. When God came to earth as a man, he allowed himself to become a perfect sacrifice to make full atonement for the sins of the human race. To take advantage of this, humans had to invite Jesus Christ, the name given to God living among the people of earth, to take over their lives. In much the same way as money conferred power to obtain possessions to its owner, so Christ taking over a person's life gave them power but a different kind of power. From the time a person had committed their life to Christ, they became fully acceptable to God and a life of different quality developed.

Sadly, sin was so firmly embedded into the human personality that it still showed through, even in lives fully committed to Christ.

"Yes," explained Pastor Bergenstadt, "Even though I committed my life to Christ many years ago and now teach others to do the same, I daily have to confess the sins I can't avoid committing to God."

The Klandacians found these concepts challenging to comprehend but were able to understand the potentially corrupting power of money and the nature of sin which Pastor Bergenstadt had confessed infected him even now. However, up until that point, the Klandacians had not had revealed to them the extent of the devastating sin which was rampant in the world. As the days continued and more of the world's culture was revealed to them, they became aware of the depravity which existed in some places.

The Klandacians were able to use their handkerchief computers to show images and films of life on Klandacia. Pastor Bergenstadt in turn was able to illustrate with films and videos what life was like beyond his small village in the rest of the world. Much of what he could show them, the scenery, great buildings, fine choirs and prestigious orchestras was beautiful, the very finest earth had to offer, but he didn't shrink from showing them the other side of humanity. They were noticeably shocked by films and documentaries depicting war and crime, marital infidelity and cruelty.

"Learning about life in Klandacia may help the people on earth to see what life should be like," said Pastor Bergenstadt, "and I hope that this may be something you will be able to teach them while visiting earth."

The impact of the recent Coronavirus on the earth's population and its economic impact from which the world was reeling was described. Pastor Bergenstadt explained the steps his church had taken to offset some of the financial problems members of his church were facing.

Gavilhem pointed out that what had been explained to him as economics was not a science recognised on Klandacia.

"Because we are a cashless society and our greatest wish is to be of service to those around us, the economic problems you are experiencing on earth just didn't arise when we had a similar pandemic on Klandacia," he explained. "However, you have told us of how your church has dealt with the problem. If similar things are being done in other communities, the economic consequences of the pandemic should be short-lived."

Pastor Bergenstadt then sadly explained that other communities were not doing what his church had done. They had been considerably helped to meet this crisis in the way they did through being Christian and following God's teaching in their holy book, the Bible.

"However," he pointed out, "Christianity was only one of several world religions and many who profess to be Christians fall far short of Christian ideals. People love their money so much that they are reluctant to voluntarily part with it."

The Klandacians realised that they had left Klandacia twelve years earlier long before the Coronavirus outbreak on earth. God had clearly timed their journey in anticipation of their need to reach earth just after this devastating pandemic.

As Pastor Bergenstadt took counsel with the elders of his church, they recognised that the Klandacians had not just been sent to their community but had important intelligence to share with the rest of the world. Czech (Bohemian) would not be an efficient language to fulfil this purpose. They needed to be able to speak one of the world's major languages. It was decided that they should be taught English before making contact with the worldwide community. There were two members of Pastor Bergenstadt's church who taught English at a local school and at an evening institute and their services were recruited to provide this tuition. Coming from a monolingual planet, the Klandacians were surprised that different languages were spoken on earth but they set to work with a will and enthusiasm to learn this additional language which they realised they would need to communicate with the world at large. There were plenty of good films available in video form in the English language to assist in this study and the Klandacians surprised their teachers by quickly becoming fluent in English, even being able to speak it without the trace of an accent.

Chapter 8

The Klandacians are introduced to the World

After six weeks had passed, Pastor Bergenstadt convened a meeting with the elders of the church. Apart from the space capsule having been picked up by earth bound radar, there was no evidence beyond this Moravian community that the Klandacians existed. The military jets had failed to intercept the capsule which could be flown like an aeroplane and as it had been designed to effect a vertical landing, there was no obvious place that could be explored by the reconnaissance jets as a probable landing site for this unidentified flying object. It was just written off as another UFO. The local community had been faithful to Pastor Bergenstadt's instruction not to publicise the arrival of the Klandacians beyond their local community until the Klandacians had had time to acclimatise themselves to the world and its ways. Such a time had now arrived.

"Our Klandacians have fitted in so well with us and the members of our church," Pastor Bergenstadt began. "They have been really delightful company. Their ability and rate of learning has amazed us. I know that we would like to keep them with us forever. However, we must consider what God's intentions might have been. They obviously have a great deal to share with the world at large and God has clearly sent them to help the world out of the post pandemic depression which the world is now experiencing. Remember, they too have experienced a similar pandemic on their own planet of Klandacia. This will be an important experience for them to share with the world. What might be the best way to bring the Klandacians to the attention of the world at large?"

Hermanschel, a local store owner, made the first suggestion.

"We simply need to contact the press. The place will soon be swarming with journalists."

This suggestion was not widely approved. It evoked visions of swarms of journalists, clamouring round the Klandacians for interviews and climbing over and into the space capsule which was still in the middle of the square but protected with a tarpaulin cover secured by heavy weights placed around its perimeter. They would be taking photographs which many would not wish to see appearing in sensation seeking daily papers. The journalists would be followed by flocks of tourists. This was not the way they wished the Klandacians to be introduced to the world beyond their small Moravian community.

Kauffmann, a fairly senior civil servant, spoke next.
"I have a friend of a friend of a diplomat who sits at the United Nations Assembly. I think that introducing the Klandacians to the world through the agency of the United Nations would be the most judicious way of proceeding. It would protect them against exploitation by any commercially orientated enterprise and I think we must trust to the collective wisdom of the world's statesmen on how to take advantage of what the Klandacians have to offer the world."

Everyone agreed with this suggestion. A few days later, the diplomat arrived with a small team of United Nations bureaucrats to meet the Klandacians.

By and large, they were very impressed. One member of the team was sceptical however. The arrival of an extra-terrestrial space craft carrying these people just didn't seem credible. Yes, they had been shown what looked like a space capsule. Yes, the Klandacians had six fingers and toes on each hand and foot and were clearly different from the rest of humanity, but couldn't this thing be just an elaborate hoax, taking advantage of four gifted but nonetheless freakish humans? After all, wasn't there a Biblical character from Rapha in Gath who had six fingers and toes on each hand and foot? *(2 Samuel ch 21 v 20)*

This delegate had quite a shock when he looked around and saw Gavilhem talking to a black member of the delegation. Gavilhem had turned black himself! Up until that time, the Klandacians had looked Caucasian, just like the people among who they were dwelling, but this Klandacian could metamorphosise himself into a black person! It was explained that when two Klandacians were speaking with one another, their colour changed until they became the same colour as each other. Clearly, when a Klandacian was speaking to a human, only the Klandacian's colour could change to match the human's. This settled the matter. The Klandacians were genuine and steps should be put in hand to enable them to address the United Nations Assembly.

Thus it was, arrangements were made to fly the Klandacians to Geneva. A silence fell over the General Assembly of the United Nations as the Klandacians were introduced and Bramensel rose to speak. She spoke in English but of course, her words were translated into the languages of all who were present. They listened intently through their headphones. Of the four of them, Bramensel had not only learnt to speak English fluently with no trace of an accent but could emphasise her words and pause in appropriate places as well as any orator, experienced at speaking in English. Her speech came over as both natural and compelling.

Bramensel started by telling them about Klandacia and illustrated her talk with pictures and film which had been downloaded from the Klandacians' handkerchief computers. She described the devastating impact of the narcolepsy epidemic on the population but explained that in that cashless society, the pandemic brought no devastating economic repercussions. Bramensel proudly explained that this had largely come about because the dearest wish of each and every Klandacian was to live, not for themselves, but for the benefit of those around them. The Klandacians all felt a genuine and sincere love for all those who shared life on their planet, and that as they served one another, she knew they were serving God. She didn't say 'our God' because as far as the Klandacians were concerned, God was God of the universe and that included the planet earth where they were now living. Bramensel told the assembly that during her short time living on earth, she had learnt about earth economics and recognised that there was no way that the planet could continue to operate without continuing to base its commerce on cash transactions. However, one thing she had learnt through the society in which the Klandacians had been living since their arrival on earth, was that if those with enough were prepared to voluntarily give to those who had lost so much, life could quickly be brought back to normal.

Not only was the Assembly impressed by Bramensel's address but they were amazed at the pictures and films Bramensel had shown them of Klandacia. They almost gasped in awe at the great subterranean towns. They were intrigued by a film of passball, the Klandacian equivalent of a football match, played on a hexagonal pitch. They recognised that Klandacian technology was well ahead of the earth as they saw pictures of driverless cars and vertical take-off aircraft. They admired the beautiful buildings which served the whole community and which had been built above the subterranean towns and cities. They marvelled at the series of pictures which illustrated how a vast Klandacian desert had been converted step by step into fertile land which could support farming, allow the grazing of wild herbivores on vast plains and accommodate huge rain forests. This had been possible because the establishment of fertile land which supported plant life had caused a dramatic local climate change and rainfall was now plentiful in that region. The delegates from desert bound states recognised that such a transformation might be possible in their own countries.

At the end of this impressive talk, the General Secretary announced the course of action which he had already decided would be the best way to follow up this amazing revelation. He knew that had he opened the meeting to questions, there would be insufficient time to allow every delegate to ask the many questions which must have been flooding through their minds. Instead, he suggested that during their stay on earth, the Klandacians should spend time in the different countries which constituted the United Nations. In the case of small countries like the Benelux states, they would need to share a visit, otherwise the Klandacians would not be able to complete their world tour during the year which was the scheduled duration of their stay on earth. It had to be understood that the Klandacians were needed back on their own planet and their loved ones back home would be considerably older on their return in view of the fact that the journey between Klandacia and the earth took several years.

The Assembly dispersed with the delegates talking excitedly among themselves. The Klandacians were delighted to see that Bramensel's address had been so well received. This augured well for their forthcoming world tour. At this stage in their mission, they were just beginning to become really homesick. They'd never been away from their families for so long before but they now felt heartened. The job they had really come to do was about to start.

Chapter 9

The World Tour

The Klandacians started their tour visiting the main European countries which included Sweden, Norway, Russia, Germany, France, Spain, Italy and the Benelux countries. They were entertained with guided tours round the main sites of beauty and interest in these lands. They were also taken to see the huge war graves in parts of Belgium and France and were appalled to see the unnecessary loss of life occasioned by war. War was unknown in Klandacia.

In their addresses to these nations, the Klandacians covered the same ground that Bramensel had presented to the United Nations. They were pleased to discover that many communities were already doing what the Moravian community, which had been their first hosts, were doing but, sadly, these were in the minority by far. They completed their tour of each country in the hope that what they had shared would be taken to heart.

They had had to communicate via a translator as they visited these European countries but really felt at home as they visited Great Britain and Ireland as they found they could converse easily and naturally with the inhabitants in a language they had learnt well while with the Moravians through their amazing linguistic skills and the excellent teaching they had received. Their time was shared between London, Edinburgh, Cardiff, Belfast and Dublin.

When in London, they were impressed by the Houses of Parliament, Westminster Abbey, St. Paul's Cathedral and the Tower of London. They had visited great castles during their time on mainland Europe and were rather shocked that such buildings and their purpose had been a necessary part of the way earth's society had developed. Early on during their visit, they were introduced to the Queen and the Duke of Edinburgh in Buckingham Palace. Monarchy, and indeed aristocracy, were unknown echelons of society in Klandacia but their role and their importance in the way earth's society had developed had been explained to them during the time they had spent with the Moravian community. The Klandacians were amazed that even the Secretary General of the Klandacian Council of Nations didn't live in a house as grand as Buckingham Palace.

As they toured London, they were surprised that so many monuments were there to commemorate war lords such as Nelson, Wellington and the like. They were specially interested in the statue of Richard Coeur-de-Lion (King Richard I) outside the Houses of Parliament and were surprised that he had actually spent very little time in England, most of his life being occupied by the crusades, wars to prevent the land where Jesus Christ was born from being taken over by the forces of Islam.

They really took a liking to the statue of Eros above its lovely fountain. Only one of the guides conducting them round could explain why it was there. When they discovered what the monument represented, they were surprised that so few of their guides seemed to be acquainted with its significance, while they all knew about the war lords! Eros and its associated fountain was, of course, erected in memory of the Earl of Shaftesbury, the Victorian philanthropist who was responsible for replacing child labour with school education. Why Eros, a pagan God? Eros was the Greek god of love, an appropriate symbolic memorial for a man like the Earl of Shaftesbury who had demonstrated great love for the deprived members of his society.

They were taken on a tour of Imperial College and were so impressed with the work being done that they felt they needed more than a snapshot visit. Thus, they spent a couple of days meeting the academics and viewing the research facilities there. Although Klandacian technology was well ahead of that on earth, there were some projects which were very close to or even ahead of Klandacian research. Some of the areas of research were of particular interest to them.

Work being done on solar driven catalytic conversion of carbon dioxide into fuels and chemicals was related to the Klandacian technology which was behind the conversion of the carbon dioxide they breathed out, when on their space craft, into an edible product A very ambitious project was an attempt to detect the process which would turn light into matter. Time was a topic of particular interest to the Klandacians and an investigation into quantum clocks paralleled similar work being carried out on Klandacia. The advances being made in bio-printing technology was also of interest to them. Karvilsel, who was the physicist and computer science expert of the quartet, realised that the development of cyber physical systems being carried out at the college was following a significantly different route from similar research being carried out on Klandacia. Karvilsel was able to provide a considerable boost to the work being done on electrical energy transmission as she could share her knowledge on the way super conductors which worked at room temperature had already been created on Klandacia. She was able to give a lead on how such materials might be developed out on earth.

Another area which the earth scientists had been struggling with for many years was the generation of electrical power by nuclear fusion. Here again, the Klandacians were able to suggest steps which might be taken to replicate such generators which had been in use in Klandacia for some years.

At last, their time in Europe had to come to a close enabling them spend a fair allocation of time in other countries which were clamouring to be visited. They made the trans-Atlantic crossing to the United States of America by jet. It was explained to them that in the recent past, this journey could have been taken in a supersonic aircraft but such planes were no longer now operational. Karvilsel, the computer

In America, they were impressed by the skyscrapers of New York. These were reminiscent of pictures they had seen of Klandacian buildings before Klandacian, cities of this importance all been reconstructed to exist in vast subterranean caverns. An obligatory time was spent in the White House, meeting the President. They learnt more than they had already been taught by the Moravians about American history, of how it had fought a war to gain independence from Britain, and of how a great civil war had been fought to keep the country united and this resulted in the end of slavery in America. The American achievement of landing a man on the moon was not emphasised as it seemed trivial in comparison to the advanced state of Klandacian space technology. The main monuments which were brought to their attention were those of George Washington and Abraham Lincoln.

Karvilsel was amazed to learn about the devastating impact of the drug culture on young people. Like so many of us, she failed to understand how young people should allow themselves to be hooked on drugs as they surely must have known, not only the devastating affect it would have on their health, but that the cost of the drugs on which they would become addicted would be raised to beyond their ability to pay for them.

It was explained to Karvilsel that much of the drug traffic came through the porous southern border of the United States. American government scientists had hacked into computers of a South American country and discovered that its government was in league with the drug barons who perpetuated this trade. This vile trade represented a source of revenue for this South American nation. The nation of course denied any such culpability but apart from obtaining this information by hacking, the United States government cyber scientists had been unable to provide conclusive proof of the origin of their evidence or to do anything about the computer which was facilitating this trade.

Karvilsel had some expertise in understanding the working of Klandacian computers and wondered if she could help with this problem. She was quickly able to understand the type of programme which was being used and beyond that, she realised the sort of operating system being used. Binary counting was common to both earth and Klandacian computers. This had provided a useful starting point for Karvilsel to learn about the operating systems of earth computers. When she explained that she recognised the type of operating system being used to the cyber scientists who were working on the problem, they realised that the operating system had been imported from somewhere in Silicon Valley in the first place. They were able to obtain details of this operating system from the original suppliers. Karvilsel then showed them how the operating system could be tweaked to change any number which had been keyed in by a random number, five minutes after it had actually been entered. Making this change in the operating system rather than in an actual computer programme would make this problem very difficult to rectify. The change that Karvilsel had shown could be installed into the computer's operating system was a bug, resident in just one computer, rather than a virus which could spread and infect other computers. Within days, reports were received that this South American country was having great difficulty in administering its affairs due to computer problems.

After spending some time in the United States, the Klandacians also carried out successful visits to Canada, Australia and New Zealand where they projected much the same message as they had in Europe and the United States. They were also welcomed in many African countries and here, one of the physical differences between humans and Klandacians worked very much to their advantage. As they met with the black Africans, they themselves appeared black and hence, were not suspected of being agents of the white races who in the past had colonised and exploited the continent.

Many of the Asian countries were wary of inviting the Klandacians to visit their countries. The reasons were partly religious and partly political. The Klandacians were monotheistic and although the Moravians knew that the God they worshipped was the same as their own, the Klandacians were not Christian which would have otherwise disqualified them from teaching in hard-line Islamic states. As they were not Christian and their teaching was not fundamentally contrary to the ethics of a good Moslem, some of these countries welcomed them in. They were also invited to visit India in spite of the fact that the Hindu religion is polytheistic and not really in line with the Klandacian religion. However, most thinking Hindus regard their gods as being more like angels serving a supreme God rather than their being independent deities like the pagan gods of the ancient Greeks and Romans. Vishnu or Ishvara, identified with Krishna, is the supreme Hindu god.

They were not invited to visit China where the Coronavirus pandemic had started. The Chinese communist rulers were atheistic and afraid that the Klandacians would provide impetus to the growing Christian church in China which they already regarded as a threat. However, news of the Klandacians and what they were saying on their tour couldn't be hidden from the Chinese people. The Klandacians and the message they were proclaiming to the rest of the world did indeed provide positive impetus to the Chinese church.

Chapter 10

An Encounter with Islamic Extremists

In a sparsely furnished hut set in a compound near Jawhat, Ibrahim al Mawli al Nurhussain was holding counsel with his lieutenants. Jawhat was a town in Somalia a few miles north of Mogadishu. Ibrahim was the leader of the remnant of a group of ISIL (Daesh) fighters who had been driven out of Syria where they had conducted a reign of terror and cruelty for some years. Although the compound was mainly occupied by members of ISIL, there were also in this compound representatives of al Qaeda, Boko Haram, Hezbollah, Hamas, Al Shabaab and the Taliban. They would sit around the compound, nursing Kalashnikovs as if carrying these weapons conferred some sort of status or marked them out as heroes.

Ibrahim and his lieutenants were discussing what they had learned about the Klandacians from the press and from their own private sources. The three men were swarthy in appearance. They wore turbans and sombrely coloured long Arab robes.

"It seems that these Klandacians come from a planet where the technology has advanced well beyond that of earth," Ibrahim began. "They have shared some of this technology among the nations they have visited during their time here."

"What might we be able to do if we had access to such technology," observed he senior of the two lieutenants, Amir al Khilabah.

"What indeed," replied Ibrahim. "We would be able to re-establish our presence in Syria and from there, extend our influence over the rest of the world."

"Yes, but this is just wistful thinking," rejoined Amir. "There is no chance that we could acquire such technology."

"I think that we just might," continued Ibrahim. "The Klandacians will be shortly visiting Pakistan. If we could capture them, we would be able to tap into their expertise."

"And just how might we achieve that?" queried Amir.

"I have discovered that the Klandacians itinerary when they visit Pakistan will include Islamabad, Multan, Hyderabad and Karachi," explained Ibrahim. "We have a good following in Pakistan. They operate in secret but they could be recruited to capture the Klandacians when they are in Karachi. I can have a helicopter waiting nearby which will conduct them to a private airstrip from which we have operated before. From there, they can be airlifted here to Somalia."

Ali Bakr al Kaunsaa, the other lieutenant then spoke.

"What you suggest is hardly in line with the teaching of the Koran," he ventured. "Will we really be able to recruit faithful ones to carry out this venture? I can't imagine that this could take place without bloodshed and most of those killed will be good Moslems."

Ibrahim had often been irritated by Ali Bakr's caution but Ali Bakr was a good officer to have in the field when there was fighting to be done.

"Bah!" was Ibrahim's contemptuous reply. "How many of our followers really know what's in the

Koran? Even the Arabic speakers have difficulty in deciphering its teaching. Those of other tongues may have attended madrasas as kids but you don't learn enough Arabic there to read the Koran. The kids spend their time learning to recite great chunks of the Koran in Arabic and they don't understand what they are reciting anyway. No, our people just rely on the mullahs to tell them what's right or wrong. There's nothing like telling people that what they are doing is service to God to encourage them to do things which they might otherwise consider to be wrong. Since when did we worry about killing other Moslems in our cause? We've slaughtered hundreds if not thousands in Syria."

Ibrahim paused to contemplate what might be achieved.

"I gather from a source in Washington that the Klandacians have enabled the Americans to take control of the computers of the government of a South American state which were used to carry out national administration. If we could capture the Klandacians, they could enable us to take over key computers of other countries. If we controlled the Pentagon computer and the Russian equivalent, we could arrange for them to 'nuke' each other."

 Ibrahim chuckled at this evil design.

"If Russia and America go to war, we could occupy the power vacuum left when they destroy each other."

The Klandacians' visit to Pakistan went ahead as planned. The time spent in Islamabad, Multan and Hyderabad was very profitable. Like most other nations, Pakistan was suffering the severe economic downturn caused by the pandemic. Although the Klandacians were hardly a Moslem source of authority, what they said about the advantages of the wealthy going beyond the bounds of mere generosity to help those who had become destitute as a result of the pandemic made sense. The people went away from these meetings to consider just how such help could be put into effect in their communities.

The meeting in Karachi had started well. It was taking place in the evening as night was drawing in. Suddenly, the main lights were extinguished, leaving just faint emergency lighting. Shots rang out. A few men rushed forwards to the Klandacians telling them,

"Come with us, your lives are in danger!"

These guides knew of a back entrance to the Meeting Hall. Once outside where the street lighting enabled them to see what was going on, Bramensel and Gavilhem and two other people they didn't know found themselves being conducted away from the Meeting Hall by a small group of armed men. When they were some way away, they paused while the armed men took stock of the situation they were now in. They had obviously expected to be leaving the Hall with all four Klandacians.

"You're not Klandacians!" they said in Urdu to the other man and woman who had been hustled out with Bramensel and Gavilhem.

"Indeed, we're not!" was their indignant reply.

"Come with us," said two of the armed men and they moved off with the couple in a different direction while Bramensel and Gavilhem continued along the road with the rest of the group. After a while, two shots were heard to ring out. A short time later, both of these armed men re-joined the group without the man and woman with whom they had left earlier.

Bramensel and Gavilhem now realised what was happening. They were being abducted. They recognised the significance of the shots they had just heard. They had very soon realised during their time on earth that the morality of humans was not the same as that of Klandacians and they had understood Pastor Bergenstadt's explanation for this but they hadn't previously encountered deep menacing evil of the sort which confronted them now. For the first time during their visit to earth, they felt fear. A quality looked for in selecting Klandacian astronauts is their ability to remain calm in dangerous situations without displaying signs of fear which could have a bad effect on the morale of members of their team. Bramensel and Gavilhem remained outwardly calm and realised that for the time being, it was in their interests to behave as if they trusted the men who were conducting them to some unknown destination.

They came to a clearing where a helicopter was waiting with its engines running and were ushered aboard. The helicopter took off, landing a short time later at an airstrip. Bramensel and Gavilhem were transferred to a small plane which they boarded with a couple of the armed men and it took off. They were wise enough not to speak to each other while in this situation with men intent on evil. A few hours later they landed. They were in Somalia. A jeep was waiting and this took them to the compound which was Ibrahim al Mawli al Nurhussain's headquarters. Dawn was beginning to break.

"Welcome to our humble dwellings," he said with an obsequious bow as he came out from his hut to meet the Klandacians as they alighted from the plane. "Thank goodness you're safe," he said in English.

He looked at the group with an anxious expression.

"Where are the other two?" he barked in Arabic.

One of the men who had been with them from the time they were abducted spoke up, looking very shame faced.

"In the confusion when the lights went out, they managed to get two ordinary people to stand where the Klandacians had been. It wasn't until we were well clear of the building that we discovered what had happened." he said, trying to put as blameless a slant as he could on what had taken place to explain why his mission hadn't been completely successful.

"Where are these people?" said Ibrahim in an aggressive tone.

"They were dealt with," said the terrorist, using a euphemism which Ibrahim understood.

Ibrahim now reverted to English to speak to the Klandacians.

"We fear that your friends may have been killed," he said in a level calm voice, "but you will be safe with us. We may not be able to accommodate you in the style you have enjoyed in recent weeks but the important thing is that you're out of danger. Let me show you to your sleeping quarters."

He led them to what looked from the outside like a small aircraft hanger but when they were inside, they realised that it had been divided into a number of smallish rooms. They were shown to two of these, each with a bed on which had been laid out western style clothing similar to what they had been wearing since being on earth. Each room had a washstand with an earthenware bowl. Ibrahim turned on the tap for a few seconds to indicate that water was available. In that climate, it was not cold but lukewarm.

"You must be hungry," he said and led them to what was a communal dining room. At the end of this room, a table for seven had been laid out. He barked an order in Arabic to two of the men standing around and they removed two of the chairs. Ibrahim and his lieutenants ushered Bramensel and Gavilhem to two of the seats and once Bramensel and Gavilhem were seated, Ibrahim and his lieutenants occupied the remaining chairs. Ibrahim clapped and Arab women came in, serving fruit juice, bread, figs and oranges.

Bramensel and Gavilhem were wise enough to say very little. They realised that these men were up to no good but had no idea as to who they were and what they were up to.

Ibrahim did most of the talking. He explained that they had been rescued from the Americans. (The Americans had organised the Klandacians visits to the other countries and the Klandacians invariably travelled accompanied by a team of Americans.) He described the United States as the Great Satan and claimed this country had used its wealth to inflict misery on the rest of the world's people but that he, Ibrahim, was leading a holy army whose intention was to destroy the United States.

Bramensel and Gavilhem had learnt enough about the current state of the world during their time on earth to suspect that they were in the hands of Arab terrorists who had done such evil things in Syria. Their suspicions were soon to be confirmed.

Ibrahim was well aware that the Klandacians had not slept during their journey from Pakistan to Somalia and although it was now only midmorning, he suggested that they should go to their rooms to rest. They were dismayed when they were told that they had to be locked in their separate rooms for their own safety but they had a resource of which Ibrahim was completely unaware.

Once locked in their rooms, Gavilhem took out his handkerchief computer which doubled up to be used in many technical ways including functioning as a phone. He contacted Bramensel by text, realising that it would be unwise to speak out loud and alert these Arabs that they were able to communicate with each other. They had both come to the same conclusion about the people who had brought them here but they didn't know where they were or why except that they were sure that it was for no good reason.

"We must try and contact the others to ascertain that they're all right and find out what they can tell us about what happened last night," he texted to Bramensel. "I just hope we can use the internet and make radio contact."

Gavilhem was lucky. He was able to get through to Stanilhem and Karvilsel on his handkerchief computer and they communicated by text. Stanilhem and Karvilsel were relieved to find that for the moment, Gavilhem and Bramensel were safe but they stressed to them that they were in great danger. Yes, they were in the hands of Daesh terrorists. The previous night, the lights had been out for several minutes and when they came on again, Gavilhem and Bramensel were gone and several people who had shared the stage with them had been shot!

"We don't know where you are," texted Stanilhem, "but the Americans we are with are sure that a rescue can be effected if we can discover your location. When you next text, give us as much information as you can about your environment. Meanwhile, don't antagonise your captors but pretend to play along with them."

They replied with a reassuring text to complete the communication and Gavilhem and Bramensel tried to get some sleep. Although they were anxious, they were also extremely tired and sunk into a deep sleep. It was early afternoon when they awoke to a tapping on the door which was unlocked and they were greeted by a smiling

Ibrahim. I trust you have slept well. You probably feel in need of exercise.

They walked out of the compound, where a number of Arabs were lazing around and doing nothing in particular, to a nearby town on the banks of a river. Apart from the river, there were no other obvious geographical features which might enable their location to be identified. They went into a shop which seemed to be a sort of general store. Ibrahim and his lieutenants went around the counters, picking up the things they needed to purchase. Bramensel and Gavilhem looked sufficiently similar to everybody else milling around in the shop and didn't attract attention. Bramensel picked up a newspaper which lay discarded among other litter on the floor and unobserved by the three terrorists, she concealed it under her tunic. On their way back, they said little but Ibrahim tried to be pleasant, pointing out trees and spectacular flowering plants which he thought might have been of interest to the couple. Every now and then, small animals scurried into the undergrowth at the sound of approaching humans. Some brightly coloured butterflies occasionally fluttered by.

On their return to the compound, they were served with another meal and after this, Ibrahim came up with a specific request which he hoped the Klandacians could fulfil. He claimed that it was important for him to be able to take over the American government's computers to prevent them wreaking more suffering on the world and ushered them into his office where a laptop computer lay open on a table.

"See what you can do with this," he suggested and left them to examine the device.

Ibrahim realised that in trying to meet his request, they would log on to the internet and if they searched for news, they would read about their abduction. However, they were monotheistic like Moslems and therefore worshipped one God whom he would tell them was called Allah by Moslems. The western Christian environment where the Klandacians had spent most of their time while on earth was tertheistic, worshipping three Gods in a family they called Trinity (Such was Ibrahim's ignorance of Christianity). When this was explained to the Klandacians, Ibrahim considered they would choose to identify with Moslems rather than Christians.

Bramensel and Gavilhem discovered that the computer was in good working order. From the very significant amount they had already learned about earth computers during the time they had spent on the planet, they found that this one had been loaded with an out of date Windows operating system, the Microsoft Office package and various other bits of software they didn't recognise. Some was Arabic. It was connected to the internet. They fiddled around with the computer for a while, discovering as much as they could about the device and searching out whether it might contain some clue as to their whereabouts and what was happening to them, As Ibrahim had expected, they discovered the news about their abduction.

They emerged from the office and informed Ibrahim that they might be able to comply with his request but it would take some time. Meanwhile, they claimed they were tired and would like to return to their rooms. Ibrahim smiled. He was pleased with this response and glad that they hadn't mentioned that they had read news of their abduction. They returned to their separate rooms but this time, they weren't locked in.

Chapter 11

Plans to effect a Rescue

Once in their rooms, Gavilhem and Bramensel opened up their handkerchief computers to communicate with each other and with Stanilhem and Karvilsel. They told them what had happened so far, including that they had been requested to take over the American government's computers! They transmitted a facsimile of the newspaper that Bramensel had picked up in the shop. They inquired about the news from the outside world.

Stanilhem and Karvilsel told them the alarming news that the American government had received a ransom demand for several million dollars, not just to release them but to keep them safe. The terrorists had informed the Americans that Gavilhem and Bramensel were confined in a building around which explosives had been installed and these would be detonated should any attempt be made to rescue them. They informed Gavilhem and Bramensel that it was therefore important that they should continue to do things which would lead these terrorists to believe that they had expertise which could be useful to them.

The American government had stalled on the request to pay the ransom, claiming that they had been inundated with similar ransom demands and were carrying out an investigation to discover which one was genuine. Stanilhem and Karvilsel asked Gavilhem and Bramensel if they could give them any information which might enable their whereabouts to be identified.

Gavilhem and Bramensel could do no more than explain that they were in a compound a short distance from a town on a river. However, they hoped that the newspaper they had transmitted might give further help. They said that they would now close their handkerchief computers and try to re-establish communication in half-an-hour.

Gavilhem and Bramensel rested as best they could during this half hour and then reopened communication. The time had been profitably spent at Stanilhem and Karvilsel's end. Their American hosts had discovered from the newspaper that had been facsimiled across that they were almost certainly in Somalia. They had further deduced that it was likely that they were being held in a compound near Jawhat. This was a couple of hours drive north of Mogadishu and was located on a river. The Central Intelligence Agency (CIA) already had knowledge of a compound just outside Jawhat which was believed to be occupied by members of a Daesh group. The American government had made available some official papers which were out of date and of no importance, but it was considered that if these could be sent to Gavilhem and Bramensel to be received on their handkerchief computers and thence transmitted to Ibrahim's computer, they could use this as evidence that they were making good progress in hacking the American Governments computer. Gavilhem and Bramensel had no idea of how long they might be held in this compound and decided to slowly leak the American government documents on to Ibrahim's laptop, using this as evidence that they were making progress in fulfilling his request.

Ibrahim examined the first document which they printed out. The subject matter was of no particular interest to him but the document had came from an American government source and was clearly genuine. He was highly delighted that Gavilhem and Bramensel had made such rapid progress in complying with his request to take over the American computers. They explained to

Ibrahim that they had done the easy part in hacking the computer but actually taking control of the computer was a much more difficult task and would take time.

Meanwhile, a dispute had arisen between the Americans and Pakistanis about how they should set about rescuing the Klandacians. The Pakistanis were distraught that such an event had taken place on their soil where they were host nation and insisted that to restore their honour, their forces should carry out the rescue. The Americans thought that the task should be assigned to their elite navy SEALs (Sea Air and Land). Doubt was expressed as to whether the Pakistanis had the expertise to launch such a mission. In the end a compromise was reached. It was finally agreed that the mission would be carried out by Pakistani forces but only their most elite soldiers should be selected and that they should first be trained by the British Special Boat Service (SBS). They would be carried to the Somalian coast by an American submarine and landed by boat at night. It was realised that an advantage of using Pakistani troops was the fact that they would be less conspicuous than British or American personnel, should they be seen moving around Somalia.

The SBS like the SAS (Special Air Service) came under the Director of Special Forces which oversaw the deployment of such prestigious units. It had an enviable world-wide reputation for success in undertaking this sort of mission. Their units consisted largely of seasoned Royal Marine Commandos. They had carried out a number of successful missions in Afghanistan which included killing the Taliban leaders Mullah Dadullah in 2007 and Mullah Abdul Matin in 2008, both at locations in Helmand province. They had seen service in Iraq, Libya and Nigeria. In 2012, a mission in Nigeria to rescue two hostages, Chris McManus the Italian, Franco Lamolinan, held by Boko Haram had not been a complete success. Although their captors had all been killed, so had the hostages in this rescue attempt. The SBS were therefore particularly aware that this operation had to be carried out slightly differently as the safety of the Klandacians was of prime importance in performing this rescue. A particular success of the SBS had been achieved in Operation Barras, a hostage rescue carried out in Sierra Leone in 2000 A.D.

The Pakistani rescue team underwent an intense course of training from senior officers of the SBS. The soldiers had been well selected and the training had been successfully completed in just three days. It had been emphasised that this was not an exercise demanding heroics. The mission would have failed disastrously if the Klandacians were lost. The safe rescue of the Klandacians was the prime objective to be achieved.

The American CIA had not been idle while the negotiations as to who would carry out the rescue were underway. Their agent in Somalia had reconnoitred from a distance the compound where it was suspected the Klandacians were held and confirmed that this was indeed the case. He also reported that every morning at about eleven o'clock, the Klandacians left the compound in the company of three Arabian looking people for a half-hour constitutional. The agent was able to provide a very clear indication of where their walk took them. This intelligence was of great value to the men who were going to attempt to rescue the Klandacians.

The rescue patrol was landed by a boat launched from the American submarine in the small hours about five days after the Klandacians had been abducted. They slept under the stars until daylight broke and then made their way to Jawhat. It was still very early morning and very few people were about. They had been fully briefed about what to expect in that town. They entered in well separated pairs. There was no need to conceal their rifles! In that strange society, it was not unusual to see men strolling around with Kalashnikovs strapped to their backs. They made their way to the positions around the compound to which they had been pre-assigned. The main group hid among the undergrowth in sight of the compound. A group of three moved on to the place identified as being near the end of the morning constitutional walk. They waited. Sure enough, Ibrahim and his two lieutenants emerged from the compound in the company of the Klandacians to start their morning walk. As soon as they were out of sight, the Pakistanis edged towards the compound. One of the Arabs in the compound must have observed something. He fired a warning shot in the direction whence he had seen movement. The Pakistanis provided answering fire. The Arabs in the compound grabbed their guns and ran to the compounds perimeter. They were mown down by a salvo from the Pakistani patrol. Suddenly, an explosion took place as the hangar in which the Klandacians had stayed blew up. This was not quite the planned course of action. An assault on the compound was not supposed to take place until the Klandacians were safe.

Ibrahim and the group had just come over the brow of a hill when the gunfire and explosion were heard. Ibrahim and his lieutenants ran back to the hilltop to see what had happened. Three shots rang out in quick succession, instantly killing the three terrorists. In rushing back to the brow of the hill, they had separated themselves from the Klandacians, meaning that they could easily be picked off without the Klandacians being endangered.

The soldiers came out of hiding and introduced themselves to the Klandacians who were looking rather stunned by what had just happened. From their communications with Stanilhem and Karvilsel, they knew that these were bona fides rescuers and had no anxiety about joining them to make their way to safety. They avoided going near the compound as they approached a prearranged rendezvous to meet up with the soldiers who had launched the attack on the compound. There was always the danger that they might have been shot at by any surviving occupants of the compound had they returned that way.

The commander of the patrol radioed the submarine which was resting on the surface some way out from the coast to report the successful accomplishment of the mission and to request a boat to meet them on shore at the location where they had landed earlier. They then made their way back to this point, avoiding Jawhat. They finally arrived back in Pakistan, amid great rejoicing.

This ended a time of considerable anxiety, for the world as a whole, yes, but specially for the Klandacians. If anything, a greater degree of anxiety was experienced by Stanilhem and Karvilsel who had a waiting role, than by Gavilhem and Bramensel who were in danger but actively involved in what was taking place in Somalia. The foursome hugged each other and laughed with relief as they were finally reunited.

Chapter 12

A Story with Two Endings

The world had breathed a sigh of relief when the news broke that the Klandacians had been rescued and were safe. Special celebrations were carried out to mark the happy outcome of their escape. The Pakistani soldiers who had carried out the rescue were warmly commended and received well-deserved medals.

Meanwhile, the Klandacians continued on their mission to the world. There were only two months left before they were due to return to Klandacia and these were spent in South America, a significant part of the globe they hadn't yet visited. Such was their linguistic ability that in spite of the pressure of the schedule they were keeping up with, they had learnt Spanish and Portuguese to add to Czech (Bohemian) and English as their repertoire of languages. These were the main languages of South America and they were able to deliver their message more powerfully and eloquently than they could have done through the medium of a translator. They spoke in stadiums to huge assembled audiences who listened to their words with rapt attention.

As a result of all that the people on earth had learnt about life on Klandacia from these four astronauts, new research was generated into finding ways of harnessing energy from the earth's incandescent core and from the energy represented by the atmospheric temperature inversion which would otherwise suddenly precipitate into destructive hurricanes and tornadoes.

Coaches of football teams set up hexagonal pitches on their training grounds and used passball (Klandacian football) as a training activity. One former football manager actually converted a disused stadium into one which was suitable for playing passball as a spectator sport. A hexagonal playing area was set up and players were recruited on free transfer, from teams where their playing careers were coming to a close, to play this new game. Investment was made into producing the electronic boots and ball which would enable automatic count to be kept of successful consecutive passes. Good audiences soon materialised to watch this spectacle and the enthusiasm evoked suggested that passball might soon be as popular as other more established spectator sports.

The nations of Mali, Algeria and Libya formed a consortium of nations which would work together with the objective of converting part of the Sahara into fertile land.

Above all, people who had been impressed by the Klandacians message, started to take serious steps to address the serious imbalance of wealth between people. This had always been there but had become much worse in the aftermath of the coronavirus pandemic.

Finally, the time came for our astronauts to return to Klandacia. They returned to the United States where a farewell rally was arranged at the Robert F. Kennedy (RFK) Stadium (formerly known as the District Columbia Stadium) in Washington. Music was provided by the New York Philharmonic Orchestra. Acrobatic displays were put on. Valedictory speeches which expressed the gratitude of the people of earth to the Klandacians were delivered. Their visit had made a great difference to the way the world overcame the recession left in the wake of the coronavirus pandemic. Television cameras relayed this spectacle around the world. People who had come through the crisis recognised the benefit of sharing their wealth beyond normal generosity, not just to the recipients of their bounty, but to themselves. Thus, the world emerged from the depression sooner and more happily than might have been expected.

The Klandacians returned to the Czech Republic, to the Moravian community where their space capsule had been safely located under a protective tarpaulin in the square. The people of that community stood in silence around the edge of the square while Pastor Bergenstadt and Margarite hugged the Klandacians, a gesture which seemed natural now that the Klandacians were familiar with the customs of the world but which the Pastor and his wife had been hesitant to use when the Klandacians first set foot among that community a year earlier.

The Klandacians wave to the people as they entered the capsule was enthusiastically returned. The capsule door was closed. After a few minutes, it powered up and set off for the orbiting space station which was also the spacecraft which would conduct them back to Klandacia. They made a safe docking and entered the station. The return journey took another twelve years and was exactly like the outward journey except that during their waking periods, these astronauts had so many special memories to share.

As they approached Klandacian space, they were able to signal their imminent return to the Space Research Centre. They settled into orbit round their home planet and successfully landed their space capsule at the Klandacian Space Research Centre Headquarters where they were met by an enthusiastic crowd. They wept with joy as they were reunited with their families. Due to the effect of relativity, their family members had aged more than the four astronauts but were still in good health. Klandacian life expectancy is much greater than that of we humans. The astronauts were particularly amused at seeing their younger siblings, now grown to a maturity beyond their own. For the foreseeable future, Gavilhem, Bramensel, Stanilhem and Karvilsel would be travelling round Klandacia, giving talks illustrated with films and pictures of their experiences on earth.

Like many Klandacians, they had decided before this mission on a life of celibacy so that they could pursue lives of service to their fellow Klandacians without distraction, but things had changed during this voyage. They had shared so much and grown so close to each other that they decided to marry on their return to Klandacia, much to the joy of their friends and families. Thus, amid great rejoicing, Gavilhem and Bramensel, Stanilhem and Karvilsel, were married at a combined service, presided over by Supreme Priest Lamethem at a great Temple.

But as the chapter heading implies, this is a story with two alternative endings. Stories have been written which show how markedly different outcomes have resulted from very small changes in the course of events, a couple meeting or just missing meeting each other, a train being caught or just missed, or a person securing a job or narrowly missing being selected. However, the difference between the story you have just read and its companion story with an alternative ending is a big one, the Klandacians arriving on earth or their not arriving.

You yourself have a part in writing the ending to the alternative story of what happened on earth after the coronavirus pandemic in the situation where the Klandacians do not arrive. In spite of the big difference in the narrative, need the outcomes be so entirely different? Will those who have plenty be generous enough to use their wealth to offset the poverty of those who have so seriously lost out as a result of this pandemic? In the story you have just read, the inhabitants of earth learnt from the Klandacian description of their way of life of the inestimable value of unselfish attitudes. However, we shouldn't need a visit from the Klandacians to teach us this. We now have the opportunity to put this into practice to the benefit of everyone.

The books published by Midhurst have been written by Dr Ray Filby who has had many years' experience of church life in a number of churches, fulfilling at various times the roles of Pathfinder Group Leader, Youth Fellowship Leader, Secretary to the Parochial Church Council, Churchwarden and Reader (Licensed Lay Minister). This experience is reflected in the stories he writes which embrace several genres, including historical fiction, short stories, Bible study, murder stories and romantic fiction. They are all available from Amazon in paperback or Kindle form.

The Sun and the Moon of Alexandria

This is a fictional biopic of Apollos, a missionary saint and one of St. Paul's co-workers. Although mentioned many times in the New Testament, little is known of the life and background of Apollos. Thus, there is scope to create a story which constructs a feasible account of Apollos' youth in Egypt, his journey to Israel, his conversion, his relationship with St. Paul, his missionary work and his marriage. The story culminates in his martyrdom. In situations where Apollos interacts with well-known Biblical characters, the narrative remains faithful to the New Testament account.

(This book is published by the Book Guild)

Parables, the Greatest Stories ever told - Retold

'The Greatest Stories ever told – Retold' focuses on the better known parables of Jesus and rewrites them as situations in modern life which correspond to the situations in Jesus' day, attempting to promote the same teaching that Jesus was giving in the original parable. Each parable is preceded by a modern translation of the original parable and followed by ten questions which are suitable for a person's private devotions or for use in the context of a group Bible study.

St. Columba's – Its Life and Its People

Churches are living organisms, each with their own distinctive patterns of life. While their members experience the same ups and downs in life as the population as a whole, their Christian faith results in their reacting to circumstances in a distinctive way.

This book is a set of short stories, some of which trace the unfolding of events which occur as part of church life, and others which recount the experience of individual church members. Readers are invited to consider the practical or ethical problems which arise in these stories and think how they themselves might have dealt with or reacted to these situations.

The Countess who should have been Queen

Margaret Plantagenet was born near the end of the Wars of the Roses. As the daughter of the brother of King Edward IV, a situation could well have arisen when she or her brother, Edward, had a claim to the throne. Margaret was not ambitious to become Queen but was happy to marry a commoner and settled as an enlightened landowner with her husband in Berkshire. Margaret became Queen Catherine of Aragon's chief lady-in-waiting and was awarded a peerage to become Countess of Salisbury. Margaret faithfully supported Catherine right through her reign and as far as she could when Catherine was sent to live in isolation after her divorce. One of Margaret's sons, Reginald, became a prominent churchman and angered the King by writing a treatise, heavily critical of Henry VIII, the way he had divorced Catherine and taken over the Church of England. Reginald was living out of reach of Henry on the continent so Henry vented his wrath on Margaret and her family.

Consequences of Immature Love

Boy-Girl, Man-Woman relationships cement our society. Because these relationships are seldom straightforward, they provide scope for an indefinite number of works of fiction. In this novel, you are invited to follow the amorous adventures of Georgina Matthews and Arthur Gray from the time they leave school and start at university until they ultimately marry the partner for whom they seemed destined from the outset.

The story told might be of special interest to a young person embarking on the minefield of love and courtship as they consider the factors which led to the success or failure of the relationships encountered in this novel. Ethical factors are involved and it is significant that a shared Christian faith led to the final happy outcome.

Soldiers, Saints and Sinners

'*Soldiers, Saints and Sinners*' is a collection of fictitious stories, featuring some of the minor characters whom Jesus encountered in his ministry. It attempts to suggest how their backgrounds might have been important in the way they led to their encounter with Jesus and the way these encounters furthered the progress of Jesus' ministry. Each story is preceded by a modern Biblical translation of the passage which recounts their appearance on the scene where Jesus was ministering and is followed by five questions which are suitable for a person's private devotions or for use in the context of a group Bible study.

The Tasks of Chronavon

When sensible twelve-year-olds, Alfred and Alice meet a mysterious angel called Chronavon in the vestry of their church, it seems someone is playing a practical joke on them. After all, angels don't just pop up in church vestries to enlist the help of two young people to journey back in time to prevent a devilish time traveller from altering the course of history. Yet it soon becomes clear that Chronavon's incredible story is true. As Alfred and Alice are whisked backwards through the centuries, they become immersed in the rich customs and costumes of the past through Henry III's troubled reign, the insecurity of Princess Elizabeth before she became Queen Elizabeth I and the Civil War between the Cavaliers and Roundheads. 'The Tasks of Chronavon' is an exciting, informative tale for young readers which effortlessly weaves fact and fiction with a sprinkling of humour and shows how little human values have changed over time.

The Evil Occupants of Easingdale Castle

Teenager, Jason, and his friends, Bill, Becky and Liz, are recruited by an unusual messenger to pit their wits against an international gang of forgers, occupying their local castle. The gang are intent on destabilising the British economy by flooding the country with forged £20 notes which could pass off as the real thing. The gang is well equipped with hi-tech machines.

It remains to be seen whether Jason and his friends, who are also technically knowledgeable, can outwit the gang.

 Technology will have advanced since this book was written and young readers are invited to consider whether they could have done better than Jason and his friends with equipment now available.

A Church like Cluedo

After graduating from college as a civil engineer, Annette Owen had hoped to work in the developing world under the auspices of a missionary society. When this door to Christian service was closed, she applied to become an ordained minister but was turned down by the selection committee. She was however able to exercise a very fulfilled ministry as a clergy wife. Unfortunately, her clergy husband had dark secrets in his life of which Annette was totally unaware until a situation arose which resulted in murder being committed. The impact of this had an unexpected effect on the course of Annette's life.

Inspector Sinclair and Sergeant Powers' most interesting cases

This account of some interesting cases solved by the detective duo, Inspector Sinclair and Sergeant Powers, is not a normal 'whodunnit' in which the murderer is not revealed until the very end when the detective reveals the clues which he or she alone has picked up to solve the case without sharing their significance with the reader until the very end.
The stories in this book are divided into sections, a list of those involved to help the reader keep track of the characters,
'the Event' which describes the situation when the murder took place,
'the Investigation' which describes the systematic way in which the detectives investigated the case and
'the Evidence' in which the crucial evidence by which a cast iron case against the murderer was built up, is reviewed.

An Insight into the Gospels and the Book of Acts

'An Insight into the Gospels and the Book of Acts' is an overview of the themes, contents, emphases, and structure of the first five books of the New Testament. While there is so much similarity in the stories and teaching in each of the gospels, this book contrasts the way each gospel is written and presented. It highlights the quite remarkable differences which exist between each of the gospels as they are directed to different audiences and have different primary objectives. The book is presented with the main content of the book appearing on the right hand (odd numbered) pages and supportive texts placed opposite the relevant passages on the left hand pages.

Puzzles, Quiz and Activities

Suitable for Social Events
Volumes 1, 2, 3 & 4

These books consist of a set of puzzles, quiz and activities which the author designed for use at a monthly social event organised by St. Michael's, Church, Budbrooke, in the Community Centre in the part of the parish known as Chase Meadow. People who have opted to take part really seem to have enjoyed these activities which are interesting rather than extremely challenging. While a good general knowledge is helpful in completing some of the activities, they are not designed to expose people's ignorance as data sheets and appropriate reference books like atlases are made available to help participants find any information needed. Thus, the activities are educational.

The socials run at Chase Meadow are not restricted to church members but all and sundry are invited as part of the church outreach. With many of the activities, a final stage often involves deciphering a phrase, quote or saying. As the socials are sponsored by the church, many of the quotes to be deciphered are Biblical texts. However, anyone choosing to use these ideas could quite easily modify the final stage and use a secular quote rather than a Biblical text to be deciphered.